50
Wittiest Tales of
BIRBAL

Retold by
Clifford Sawhney

UNICORN

Publisher
UNICORN BOOKS

F-2/16, Ansari Road, Daryaganj, New Delhi-110002
☎ 011-23275434, 23262683, 23250704 • *Fax:* 011-23257790
E-mail: info@unicornbooks.in • *Website:* www.unicornbooks.in

Branch : Mumbai

23-25, Zaoba Wadi Thakurdwar, Mumbai-401002
☎ 022-22010941, 022-22053387
E-mail: rapidex@bom5.vsnl.net.in

© **Copyright: Unicorn Books**
ISBN 978-81-7806-050-7
50 Wittiest Tales of Birbal
Edition: 2018

Printed at: Param offsetters, Okhla, New Delhi-110020

Contents

Introduction

Birbal's tales of wit and wisdom make interesting reading for adults as well as children. His encounters at Emperor Akbar's Court are legendary. This is what makes Birbal one of the most popular persons in Indian history.

Emperor Akbar (1542–1605) was an exceptional ruler. His rule led to a Golden Age in Hindustan. A liberal emperor, he allowed people to worship in their own ways. Although not educated, he was a lover of philosophy and the fine arts. Akbar chose the wisest and most talented men as ministers. These people were discovered from inside and outside his kingdom. Such exceptional men were then brought to the Mughal Court.

Nine such men earned name and fame as the *Nav Ratna* (Nine Jewels). Tansen was a legendary singer. On hearing his voice, candles were said to burst into flame. Daswant, a painter, became the First Master of the Age. Todar Mal earned fame as a financial genius. Abul Fazl was a noted historian. Fazl's brother, Faizi, was a great poet. Then there was Abud us-Samad – brilliant calligrapher (an expert in decorative handwriting or lettering) and designer of Imperial coins. Raja Man Singh was an exceptional military strategist. Mir Fathullah Shirazi was an astronomer, financier, philosopher and physician (not really in that order!).

The ninth man was the people's favourite – Birbal. Known for his cleverness, generosity and sense of fair play and justice, Birbal was a *wazir* (minister). Birbal's duties were largely administrative and military. Although 14 years older, he became a close friend of Akbar. This was because the Emperor loved his wit, wisdom and gentle humour.

Birbal survived countless murder plots. He finally died fighting, while leading an expedition in northwest India. This happened in February 1586 when the Mughals tried to conquer an Afghan tribe. For days, Akbar was inconsolable on hearing of his friend's death.

Birbal's real name was, Mahesh Das. Mahesh was born in a poor Brahmin family of Tikawanpur on the banks of the Jamuna River. Thanks to his sharp wit, he rose to become a *wazir* in the Mughal Court. An accomplished poet too, Birbal wrote under the pen name, Brahma. A collection of his poems is still preserved in the Bharatpur Museum.

Birbal's close friendship with Akbar earned him many enemies. Some courtiers constantly plotted his downfall. Countless stories have been spun around these plots. It is doubtful whether most Akbar-Birbal stories actually occurred. Except for a few, the others are largely creations of village storytellers. These stories were passed on from generation to generation. And the legend of Birbal grew. Most of the stories are placed in Agra (the first capital of the Mughal Empire) and Fatehpur Sikri (which Akbar built as his capital between 1570–86).

Unicorn Books presents 50 Birbal stories in this collection for children.

—**Clifford Sawhney**

Akbar and Birbal's First Meeting

In ancient times, customs were very different. Besides a regular Court, the Mughal ruler Akbar had a Mobile Court too. The Court moved from village to village, town to town and city to city, giving justice.

One day, the Mobile Court was in a small village in today's Madhya Pradesh. In this village lived a young Brahmin farmer, Mahesh Das. Mahesh heard the village crier announce that Akbar was coming. The Badshah would award 1,000 gold coins to the artist who drew the most realistic picture of him. This was a huge amount. Mahesh thought: 'My life will change if I win this award.' But how was this possible?

Dozens of artists reached the Mobile Court the day Akbar arrived. Each artist had a covered picture. One by one, the artists simply revealed their portrait to the

9

Emperor. Sitting on a high throne, Akbar inspected each portrait.

Standing in the queue, Mahesh Das studied Akbar's reactions. Different expressions crossed the Emperor's face: a frown, a scowl, an angry look, amusement, indifference etc. Akbar's comments also differed after each look. Only if the Emperor smiled would someone win the award.

Finally, Mahesh Das walked up to present his portrait. By now Akbar was bored with the bad pictures: "Are you also an incapable artist? If so, don't waste my time! I want to see a portrait that shows me exactly as I am. Not pictures that show me younger, fairer or handsomer. I want an honest drawing."

Hearing these words, Mahesh Das broke into a smile. The Emperor was surprised by the lad's confidence. The courtiers were astonished. How could this boy be so confident of his skills?

"Have a look. Then decide for yourself, Your Majesty," Mahesh replied, still smiling.

From the folds of his garment, Mahesh produced an oval object. He quickly handed this to the Emperor. Akbar held it up. He was instantly puzzled. He looked at the "portrait" for a few seconds. Then he burst out laughing.

"Young fellow, you are very smart for one so young! Although not a portrait, this is an exact likeness of me," the Emperor smiled. Akbar then raised the "portrait" high. All the assembled people now had a look. It was a mirror!

"I award the 1,000 gold coins to this boy," the Emperor announced. "Although not an artist, he used his brains to present a carbon copy of my face."

The assembled people instantly cheered and clapped. "What's your name, my boy?" Akbar enquired.

"Mahesh Das, Sire," replied the boy.

"Mahesh, you are very clever. When you grow up, you must visit my capital, Fatehpur Sikri. Here, take this ring. It has my Royal Seal. Bring this along with you. I will always know who you are. Even if you come years later," the Emperor said.

Mahesh was overjoyed. "Thank you, Your Highness," the boy said, bowing. "I will meet you some day in your Court."

This was how the first meeting between Mughal Emperor Akbar and Mahesh Das took place. Many years later, Mahesh would earn fame as the legendary Birbal.

The Royal Seal

For years, Mahesh Das dreamt of becoming a big man. So he told his mother about his dream. He wanted to visit Fatehpur Sikri, then the capital city of the kingdom. "There," Mahesh told his mother, "I will meet the Badshah. I could then do something big and realise my dreams."

Mahesh's mother felt sad. She would lose her son if he went to Fatehpur Sikri. But she wanted him to fulfil all his dreams. So she took out her life's savings. Counting these few copper coins, she gave them to Mahesh. She then blest him and wished him luck. With this, he could reach the big city and try his luck.

Mahesh placed a small bundle of clothes on his shoulder. The young man then kissed his mother goodbye. Hidden carefully amongst the clothes was the ring with the Royal Seal, given to him by Akbar years ago.

Mahesh breathed the cool early morning air deeply. He took big steps as he walked on the road to Fatehpur Sikri.

He walked endlessly for many days. Finally, he reached the borders of the capital city. As he entered the market, young Mahesh was very excited. He had never seen a market with such colourful goods. The eating-houses along the road were stocked with various delicious foods. Most of these he had never tasted before.

The people in the city were also very well dressed. Red, yellow, orange, green, blue... there was a sea of colours all around. People galloped across on horseback. Camels walked past lazily. An elephant came ambling down the road. People quickly made way for the huge animal! A street magician was showing a crowd his bag of tricks. Water sellers called out to thirsty travellers, asking them to drink a glass of cool refreshing water.

Mahesh wondered, 'Why didn't I visit the city years before.' Thoughts of one day living a comfortable life flashed past his mind. So he walked faster towards the palace! After going a mile, he saw a big, ornamental gate. 'Perhaps,' Mahesh thought, 'this is the door to Akbar's palace.'

As he reached the huge gate, an armed guard blocked his way. "O you village bumpkin!" the guard bellowed. "Where do you think you're going? You cannot enter the Imperial City just like that."

"Why not?" asked Mahesh in his usual bold manner. He now realised this was merely the outer gate of the city.

"Do you have any official reason for a visit?" the guard asked. He twirled his long moustache threateningly.

"Oh, I do! Badshah Akbar invited me to meet him," Mahesh smiled.

"Oh, he did? That's why he always kept asking about you! He's been wondering why you hadn't turned up all these years!" the guard scowled. Then he waved his spear angrily. "Get out of here, you idiot! Do you think the Badshah meets fools?"

Mahesh pleaded, "Listen, if Badshah Akbar hears you didn't allow me to enter, he'll be very angry."

Hearing these cheeky words, the guard was mad with anger. "Get lost! Or I'll knock your head off!" he shouted, raising the spear.

Mahesh realised this could be his last chance. From his bundle, he quickly removed the ring Akbar had given him. When the guard saw the Royal Seal he stopped in surprise. Nobody could get the Royal Seal – unless the Emperor gave it personally.

"Surely you know this Seal?" Mahesh asked. "Now let me pass. Or you'll be in big trouble."

The guard knew he had to let the young man enter. But he took one last chance. "I can let you pass. But what will you give me?" he whispered.

"What do you want?" Mahesh asked.

"Half of what Badshah Akbar gives you," the cunning guard said.

Mahesh smiled. "Done!" he said and quickly walked inside the city gates.

"Don't forget your promise!" the guard called out, as Mahesh walked into the distance.

The roads inside were lined with swaying palm trees. Cool breeze blew across gently. Gurgling fountains spewed water in all directions. A river flowed past whispering merrily. Robins twittered in the trees. A koel called her mate repeatedly. The fragrance of roses and mogras wafted all around. This was like a dream. Mahesh felt as if he was in Paradise.

Houses inside the Imperial City were big and magnificent. Mahesh had never seen such huge homes. Some distance away, he noticed a beautiful marble building. 'This must be the palace,' Mahesh thought. Colourfully dressed courtiers entered the place in silence. At the main entrance, two sentries with spears stopped Mahesh. He quickly showed the Royal Seal. He was waved inside immediately.

Inside, there was a huge hall with hundreds of people. Some of them were seated. 'These must be courtiers,' Mahesh said to himself. Their costly clothes made this clear. Dozens of other people were standing. They wore crumpled cotton clothes. 'These must be common people,' Mahesh thought. Just like him.

Suddenly, Mahesh's eyes fell upon a man seated on a throne. There was a crown on his head. He had flowing silk robes. Mahesh realised this was Badshah Akbar. Yes, it was the same face he'd seen years ago.

As Mahesh came into Akbar's presence, the Emperor glanced at him. Mahesh prostrated respectfully. "May Your Highness rule forever!" Mahesh said dramatically.

The Emperor smiled and nodded. He was used to such statements. "Rise, young man! What is it you seek?"

"I seek nothing, my Lord. I've only come on your invitation..." so saying, Mahesh quickly produced the Royal Seal.

The Badshah looked at the Seal. He immediately recalled his first meeting with Mahesh years ago. "So the village boy has grown into a fine young man!" Akbar said. "Welcome to the Royal Kingdom. Ask whatever you desire, young man. It shall be granted."

"If you insist, Sire," Mahesh smiled, "I'd like to have 50 whip lashes!"

The Emperor was surprised. "Are you joking?" Akbar asked seriously.

"I wouldn't dare!" Mahesh replied.

"Then why do you seek 50 lashes?" Akbar asked.

"I can only disclose the reason after I get 50 lashes, Your Highness," Mahesh answered.

All the courtiers fell silent. The young man was mad, they thought. He'd soon feel sorry for this. Badshah Akbar clapped his hands. Two attendants immediately stepped forward. "We await your command, O Badshah!" they said, heads lowered.

"Fulfil this young man's request," the Emperor ordered.

Within seconds, a man stepped forward with a whip.

Mahesh knelt before him. Emperor Akbar held up his hand to indicate Mahesh should be whipped gently. Soon, the whip kept flying through the air. But the man made sure he lashed Mahesh gently. The courtiers looked on, puzzled.

The moment the 25th lash fell, Mahesh stood up. "Please stop!"

Akbar smiled, "You have realised your foolishness, is it?"

"O Badshah," Mahesh spoke hurriedly, "I've had my fair share. Now I'd like the other 25 lashes to be given as per my promise."

"Will you explain what you mean?" Akbar demanded.

Mahesh told Akbar about his promise to the guard. He was only allowed to enter after he promised the guard half of anything he received. Emperor Akbar was furious. The guard was summoned inside the Court. The man came joyfully. So the young man had not forgotten his promise, the guard thought happily.

"Whip this man 25 times. Hard!" Emperor Akbar commanded.

As the courtiers laughed, the guard received 25 painful lashes. Akbar then spoke to Mahesh: "The past few years have increased your wisdom, young man. You've taught a lesson to one corrupt man. But I want you to stay on at my Court. Use your wisdom to teach a lesson to all corrupt people. And because you are so wise, henceforth, you will be called 'Birbal'. From today onwards, you will be my royal adviser."

That's how Mahesh Das became Birbal – the wise royal adviser whom Akbar always trusted.

Story 3

Everything Happens for the Best

Birbal was always happy. Even when things went wrong! If there was any problem, he said: "All that happens, happens for the best." But sometimes Akbar got angry when Birbal spoke like that.

One day, Akbar hurt his finger while cutting an apple. Everybody sympathised with Akbar. But Birbal said: "*Jahanpanah*, all that happens, happens for the best."

Akbar raised his heavily bandaged finger: "Birbal, you fool! How can cutting my finger be good?"

"It is, Your Highness. You will only realise this later," Birbal said coolly.

The Emperor lost his temper: "Guards! Throw Birbal into prison. That will be the best for him!"

So without committing any crime, Birbal was jailed.

The next day, Akbar went hunting. Around a dozen courtiers went along. Akbar and his group killed many

17

animals in the jungle. In the afternoon, the group stopped for rest. Suddenly, Akbar spotted a deer. Getting up quickly, he chased it. Within minutes, he went some distance away from his group. Soon, he was lost. The hunting party also looked desperately for their Emperor. But they failed to find him.

Unfortunately, a tribe of savages found Akbar. They caught the Badshah and tied him up. Soon, they decided to sacrifice him to their rain god. This would ensure they received good rainfall that year. So they bathed Akbar's body for the sacrifice. While doing so, they noticed his injured finger. They immediately began whispering amongst themselves. The plan for a sacrifice was dropped. If an injured man were sacrificed, their rain god would be angry. So they were forced to release Akbar.

The Emperor quickly returned to the city. At the palace, the hunting party was waiting worriedly. They had reached many hours before and were concerned about Akbar's fate. Seeing the Emperor, everybody clapped in joy: "Long live Badshah Akbar!"

Akbar thanked God for injuring his finger. This had saved him. Then he remembered Birbal's words: "All that happens, happens for the best."

Akbar rushed to the prison and quickly released Birbal. "My friend, please accept my sincere apologies. Some savages had captured me in the jungle. But they allowed me to go only because I'd injured my finger. You were right. All that happens does happen for the best."

Birbal simply smiled and bowed before Akbar. Yet, Akbar was still puzzled about something: "Tell me Birbal, I threw you into prison. But how was this good for you? You were innocent."

"It's very simple, Sire," Birbal continued smiling. "If you hadn't thrown me into jail, I'd have accompanied you on the hunt. The savages would have then killed me, since I wasn't injured. Thanks for getting angry with me and throwing me into prison. That saved my life!"

Akbar suddenly realised the truth in the saying, *All that happens, happens for the best*. "Birbal, you are truly wise," Akbar patted him on the back.

18

The Oversmart Barber

Many courtiers hated Birbal. This was purely because he was Akbar's favourite minister. The Emperor's barber also disliked Birbal. Once, while trimming Akbar's beard, the barber thought of a wicked plan.

"Your Majesty, your father appeared in my dream last night," the barber lied.

Akbar was curious: "Did he? And what did my father say?"

"He said he had everything in Paradise," the barber continued lying. "But he had one big problem. All the people in Heaven are big bores. So he wished he had somebody like Birbal to crack jokes and make him laugh. He wondered how his wish could come true, since Birbal is still alive."

19

The barber then finished his work and left. He knew the Emperor would think of what he had said. That's exactly what happened. Akbar was confused. He couldn't do without Birbal for even one day. But how could he ignore his dead father's wish? So the Emperor summoned Birbal.

"Your Majesty, is there any problem?" Birbal asked, seeing Akbar's sad face.

"Yes, Birbal. My dead father sent a message in the barber's dream. He says he misses a wise man like you in Paradise," the Emperor looked closely at Birbal. "Would you be kind enough to go to Paradise?"

Birbal instantly knew the barber had played a dirty trick: "Your Majesty, going to Paradise is no problem. But I'll need a week's time to prepare myself."

Akbar was very happy: "That's no problem, Birbal. You can have a week's time to prepare."

Hearing this, all the courtiers were secretly happy. As for the barber, he was overjoyed. Birbal had no way to escape now. In seven days' time he would be dead!

Birbal left the Court hurriedly. He went home and dug a deep hole outside his house. This would be his "grave". But Birbal also dug a secret tunnel. This went from the "grave" to his bedroom.

A week later, Birbal was back in Court. "Your Majesty, as per your request, I've made preparations to go to Heaven. But I'd like to be buried alive outside my house. This is only to honour an old family custom. It will also be easier to reach Heaven if I'm buried alive."

The Emperor granted the request. All the courtiers and the barber couldn't wait to get things over. Before their very eyes, Birbal was buried alive. Unknown to these people, the moment his grave was covered with mud, Birbal quickly escaped via the secret tunnel.

For the next six months, Birbal stayed inside his house quietly. He never moved out of his room. His hair and beard grew very long. All his enemies thought Birbal was finally dead. This was something they had always wanted.

Six months later, Birbal emerged from his house for the first time. But nobody recognised him. When Birbal reached Court, it took Badshah Akbar a full minute to recognise his wise minister: "Birbal, are you still alive? How did you return from Paradise?"

"O Badshah, I was forced to return because of your father's request. It is really wonderful in Heaven. I did not want to come back, but..." Birbal told the Emperor.

"Then why did you return?" Akbar asked. "And what message did my father send?"

"Nothing much, Badshah," Birbal said, stroking his unshaved beard meaningfully. "Your father's very happy in Heaven. But he has one major problem."

"What's that Birbal? Tell me. I'll solve it," Akbar said eagerly.

"O Sire, like me, he too has been unable to shave his beard," Birbal said sadly. "You see, there are no good barbers in Heaven. Your father wants you to send the best barber to Heaven."

Birbal turned and looked at the barber. Emperor Akbar too motioned the barber to come over. The barber fainted, realising he'd fallen into his own trap.

The Camel's Crooked Neck

It was a cool winter morning. Akbar and Birbal were taking a walk in the royal garden. The Emperor was in a very good mood.

"Birbal, you've helped me in all difficult situations," Akbar admitted. "So I'll gift you 10 acres of land. Also, many precious jewels and other gifts. This is for your years of wonderful service."

"I'm honoured, *Jahanpanah*. That's very kind of you. Thank you," Birbal bowed in gratitude.

Many days passed. But Akbar didn't fulfil his promise. The very next day, Akbar wondered how he'd been so foolish. Fancy, promising so much to an already well-paid minister!

Birbal never forgot the Emperor's promise. Indeed, he never forgot other people's promises! Days turned into weeks. But Birbal kept quiet. Reminding Akbar about his promise would be improper.

One morning, the Emperor and Birbal were walking down the banks of the Yamuna River. A camel happened to pass by. The animal was walking with its neck at a crooked angle.

"Birbal," asked Akbar, "why is that camel's neck crooked?"

The shrewd minister quickly grabbed this wonderful chance for his own benefit. "Why, *Jahanpanah*, don't you know?" Birbal pretended to be surprised. "Any person who forgets a promise gets a crooked neck. This is God's way of reminding people of an unfulfilled promise. This camel must have also made a promise to someone. But it then forgot to fulfil it. Hence the crooked neck."

Akbar sheepishly realised what Birbal was referring too. The very next day, Birbal was granted 10 acres of prime land, many jewels and other riches.

The Pandit's Covered Pot

A proud pandit once visited the Mughal Court. Here, the Brahmin proclaimed: "Your Majesty, I'd like to test the intelligence of your ministers. Do I have your permission?"

The Emperor nodded.

"I wish to ask your wisest ministers a single question," the pandit said.

Akbar looked at his ministers. All of them were unsure about accepting the Brahmin's challenge. But each of them nodded. Anyway, there was no other option!

"Go ahead!" Akbar raised his hands.

The pandit produced a pot from his cloth bag. The pot was fully covered. He placed this covered pot in the centre of the Court. "Can anyone tell me what's inside this pot?" the pandit challenged.

There was total silence for a minute. Then the ministers began guessing in turns. "Wrong!" the Brahmin kept saying. "Wrong!" "Wrong!" "Wrong!"

This went on for five minutes. Suddenly, Birbal stepped forward. All eyes in the Court fell on the wise minister. Akbar was sure Birbal would solve the problem. But the pandit smiled wickedly at Birbal. There was no way even Birbal could tell what was inside the pot.

Without saying a word, Birbal advanced towards the pot. He flung off the cover, opened the pot and peeped inside. "Your Majesty, the pot is empty!" Birbal proclaimed triumphantly.

"But, b-bu-tt," the pandit protested. "You opened the pot. You cannot do that."

"Well," smirked Birbal, "you only asked what was inside the pot. You never said I couldn't open it! Please learn to frame your own rules properly."

The entire Court guffawed with non-stop laughter. The Emperor also roared with laughter. The pandit realised he'd made a fool of himself. He quickly bowed towards the Emperor. Then he quietly slunk away in shame and embarrassment.

The Meditating Parrot

A sadhu once gave Akbar a talking parrot. The bird could utter over a hundred words. Soon, Akbar grew very fond of the bird. He hired a special attendant for his pet. The man had to look after the parrot's every need.

The Emperor one day warned the attendant: "Make sure my pet is always fine. If any person ever gives me bad news about my parrot, I'll have him beheaded."

From this day onwards the attendant was terrified. 'If anything happens to the parrot, I'll surely be killed,' he thought. Day and night, the man stayed around the bird. He had to ensure the parrot was always fine.

A year later, the parrot died, as most birds usually do! This was purely due to old age. The attendant recalled the Emperor's threat. He went mad with fear. Before anyone knew the parrot had died, he rushed to Birbal.

"*Huzoor*, you must save me!" the man pleaded.

26

"I will save you," Birbal answered. "But only if you tell me what to save you from!"

"The Emperor's parrot died last night," the man trembled. "Now I'll be killed when I tell His Majesty the bad news."

"So don't tell His Majesty!" Birbal began laughing.

The attendant was upset: "*Huzoor*, you're laughing at my problem."

"No! I'm laughing thinking about the solution," Birbal replied.

Birbal then whispered in the attendant's ear. "Now you can relax," Birbal said.

The man calmed down. Birbal would himself convey the bad news to Akbar! But he'd do it in his own way...

"Long live the Emperor!" Birbal bowed before Akbar.

"What's the matter Birbal?" Akbar asked suspiciously. The Emperor wondered what was behind the "Long live" part. Birbal rarely spoke that way.

"Sire, your parrot turned holy. It is meditating since last night!" Birbal told the Emperor.

"Nonsense, Birbal! Even you cannot make my parrot meditate," Akbar scolded Birbal.

Badshah Akbar then rushed over to see his parrot. "As you can see, Your Majesty, the bird has closed its eyes. It's been looking heavenwards since last night," Birbal said solemnly.

"You idiot!" Akbar reacted angrily. "Can't you see my parrot is dead?"

"I can, Sire! I can!" Birbal admitted. "But then you'd have beheaded me."

"Well, I see..." Akbar stopped short. He immediately realised what Birbal had been up to. "Birbal, once again you've saved another man's head with your wisdom."

Listening in the background, the attendant silently thanked God and Birbal for saving him.

The Face That Brought Bad Luck

An old servant in Akbar's palace was said to bring bad luck to anyone who saw him first thing in the morning. One morning, the Emperor bumped into this man. For the rest of the day, bad things kept happening.

Barely minutes after seeing him, Akbar slipped and fell. Next, his grandson fell ill. Two hours later, news arrived about a revolt in some distant province. In the afternoon, Akbar had a severe headache.

By evening, the bad news kept mounting. Suddenly, Akbar remembered that the first person he saw was the old servant. 'This is all that servant's fault,' Akbar thought.

Akbar summoned his guards. "Arrest that old servant. He'll be hanged first thing tomorrow morning!" the Emperor proclaimed.

Before the guards got to the old servant, the news reached him. The man fled to Birbal's house.

"*Huzoor,* the Emperor has ordered my death. Only you can save me now," the man begged.

Birbal reassured the man and told him not to worry. He'd find a way out, as he always did.

Within minutes, Birbal was before Akbar: "*Jahanpanah,* your old servant is innocent. With your permission, I'll prove this."

Akbar had serious doubts. But he agreed to give Birbal a chance to prove his words. Birbal said he could do so if allowed to question the servant before Akbar. The Emperor consented.

The man was called before Akbar and Birbal. Then, Birbal asked the man: "Who was the first person you saw today morning?"

The servant answered fearfully: "The Emperor, *huzoor.*"

"What fate awaits you now?" Birbal asked next.

"I'll be hanged tomorrow morning," the man said tearfully.

Birbal turned to Akbar. "There, Your Highness. You saw him first thing in the morning. After that, you had many complaints. Yet, not one was life threatening. But the first person this poor man saw was Your Highness. And now he'll lose his life."

Akbar shifted his gaze downwards. It was an uncomfortable moment.

Birbal continued: "Now, in all fairness, Your Highness must decide. Whose face has led to greater misfortune? Your seeing this man's face in the morning? Or this man seeing your face in the morning?"

Birbal's point was unmistakeable. Akbar admitted his mistake. "Birbal, you're right. Nobody's face leads to misfortune. What's to happen will happen. I took a hasty decision."

The just Emperor immediately cancelled the old servant's death sentence.

A 'Twig' Tells the Truth

Many times, Akbar tried to outsmart Birbal. But he always failed. Birbal had answers to everything. This time, Akbar had a 'foolproof' plan. He called a courtier. "Keep this ring with you. Don't tell anyone about it. Return it only when I ask you to."

The courtier took the ring. The Emperor's wish was a command. He hid it in his pocket.

Later that day, Akbar called Birbal. "I lost my ring while bathing, Birbal. I'm sure a courtier stole it. You are also known for your astrological powers. Can you find the thief for me?"

Birbal hid his smile. He knew Akbar was up to some mischief. What it was would soon be clear. "Where did you place the ring before bathing, Your Highness?"

"I kept it on that cupboard," Akbar lied.

"Oh, I see," the wise minister spoke in all seriousness.

Birbal quickly walked over to the cupboard. He then pretended to question the cupboard! Akbar and his courtiers were amused. "*Huzoor*, the cupboard has named the thief," Birbal stated.

"Has it?" Akbar feigned surprise. "And whom did the cupboard name?"

"The cupboard whispered that the thief has a twig in his beard," Birbal revealed.

Without thinking, the courtier who had the ring touched his beard.

"There, Your Majesty! This is the thief," Birbal pointed to the man.

The man looked at Akbar questioningly. The Emperor smiled in acknowledgement. So the courtier quietly produced the ring. He then handed this to Birbal.

"Your wisdom is without equal, Birbal," Akbar admitted.

Well Water Rent

Akbar's Court received complaints of all kinds. Once, a farmer and his neighbour landed in Court. They had an unusual complaint.

"Your Majesty, I bought a well from my neighbour," the farmer said. "But now he wants me to pay for the water!"

"That's right, Sire. I only sold him the well. I didn't sell the well water. So what right has he to use this? If he uses the water, he must pay me for it," the neighbour insisted.

The Emperor was puzzled. He quickly asked Birbal to handle the case.

Birbal turned to the farmer's neighbour. "You mentioned that you sold your well to this farmer. Is that correct?" he asked.

The neighbour agreed this was true.

"In that case," Birbal leaned forward, "the well belongs to him now, but not the water. Right?"

Again, the man admitted this was true.

"Now," demanded Birbal, "why have you kept all *your* water in *his* well? Once you sold your well to the farmer, you should've drained out all your water. Or kept it separately with you. To settle the dispute, you'll have to pay rent for all the days you keep your water in his well! If you can't pay the rent, remove your water at once!"

The neighbour realised his trick had bounced back on him. He quickly begged forgiveness and promised never to make false claims.

Pulling the Emperor's Whiskers

The Emperor always planned new ways to test his courtiers. Today, Badshah Akbar came up with a strange question: "If somebody pulls my whiskers, how should he be punished?"

"He should be whipped a thousand times!" one courtier said.

"He should be hanged upside down!" a second replied.

"He must be hanged to death!" a third insisted.

"He must be beheaded!" a fourth added.

Birbal was silent. So the Emperor turned to him: "What punishment would you suggest, Birbal?"

"He should be given a box of sweets," Birbal said coolly.

"A box of sweets?" everybody gasped. Birbal had gone mad! The Emperor wouldn't spare such a cheeky response.

"Why do you say that?" the Emperor queried.

"*Jahanpanah*, there's only one person on earth who'd dare pull your whiskers. Your three-year-old grandson! Naturally, a box of sweets is the best 'punishment'!"

"Birbal, only you can come up with the right answers," the Emperor congratulated him. The entire Court applauded Birbal's wisdom.

The Proud Astrologer

There was a very proud astrologer. He always boasted that all his predictions came true. Akbar heard of his boast. This proud astrologer must be taught a lesson, the Emperor decided. So the man was summoned to Court.

"You claim all your predictions come true, right?" the Emperor queried him.

"Y-yes, Your Majesty," the man replied with fear. He knew the Emperor would ask him a difficult question. If he failed, he'd be in serious trouble.

"Then," demanded Akbar, "tell me when you will die!"

"Your Highness," the man trembled, "I'll need an hour to consult my charts."

"An hour is all you have!" Akbar said firmly.

Frightened, the man rushed to Birbal. He explained his problem. Whatever day he predicted he'd die on, the Emperor could prove him wrong by ordering his immediate death!

"Relax!" Birbal told the astrologer. "This is what you must tell the Emperor..." Birbal whispered something in the man's ears.

An hour later, the astrologer was in Court. "Have you discovered the time of your death?" Akbar asked.

"Yes, Sire," the astrologer spoke confidently. "As per my charts, I will die three days before Your Majesty."

Akbar was stumped. He knew the astrologer was lying. He was sure the man had consulted Birbal. But he didn't want to risk his own death after three days!

Yet again, thanks to Birbal's wisdom, a man was saved.

Six Magic Sticks

It was a scorching summer day. A rich merchant decided to have a bath. This would refresh him. So he undressed. Then he removed all the gold he was wearing. He tied this up in a bundle and left it on a table.

Ten minutes later, the merchant came out from the bathroom. When he went to the table, he was shocked. His gold was missing! He called his six servants and questioned them. But each of them denied knowing anything about the theft.

Unable to find the thief, the merchant went to Emperor Akbar. He revealed how his gold had been stolen from the table while he bathed. As usual, the Emperor assigned the case to Birbal. This was the fastest way to solve problems!

Birbal had the merchant's servants summoned to Court. When the six appeared, Birbal gave each man a stick. "These are six magic sticks," Birbal told the servants. "Each of you will take this home. And bring them back tomorrow. When kept with a thief, the magic stick will grow by one inch every day!"

All the servants took one stick and went home.

The next day, all reappeared in Court with the sticks. Birbal had each servant place his stick before him. The sticks were then measured one by one. One stick turned out to be an inch shorter.

Birbal pointed to the man. "This one is the thief!" the wise minister told the merchant. "He stole the gold. But afraid that his stick would grow by an inch, he cut an inch off to escape detection."

Then Birbal spoke to the servants: "These are ordinary sticks, not magic ones! But because you believed they were magic sticks, the guilty man cut off an inch from his stick."

The servant who stole the gold immediately fell on his knees and begged forgiveness from the Emperor. As usual, it took Birbal barely a day to solve the case.

The Brahmin's Desire

There once lived a Brahmin named Hariram. His forefathers were learned Sanskrit scholars. Therefore, people respectfully called them 'Panditji'. Hariram was a rich Brahmin. He had all the comforts of life. But he was a simple man and never bothered about his riches.

However, he had just one wish in life. He was not a very learned man. Nor was he interested in learning. Yet, he had a burning desire. He wanted people to call him "Panditji", just as his forefathers were called. But nobody called him that. Could Birbal solve his problem?

Birbal tried to convince him that such words didn't matter. But the man wouldn't agree. He wanted to be called "Panditji".

"In that case," said Birbal, "follow my instructions." Birbal told the Brahmin to tell the first boy he met, "Don't call me 'Panditji'. I don't like it." The first thing the boy

40

would do was to call him "Panditji". Thereafter, other children would hear of this. They'd then tease him saying, "Panditji! Panditji!" Each time, the Brahmin should pretend he was very offended and chase them.

The Brahmin went home. Near his house, he told the first child he saw, "Don't ever call me, Panditji. I don't like it!"

Within days, everybody was calling him Panditji. And the Brahmin always pretended to get very angry! Within a month, the entire town was teasing him, "Panditji! Panditji!"

At last, the Brahmin's dream was fulfilled.

The Real Donkeys

One summer morning, Akbar, his two sons and Birbal went to the banks of the Yamuna. Akbar and his sons decided to take a bath. Since Birbal had already taken a bath, he waited by the riverbank. So Akbar asked Birbal to hold their clothes and wait there.

Some time later, the Emperor looked at Birbal. With their clothes slung over his shoulder, he looked really funny. Akbar decided to poke fun at Birbal.

"Hey, Birbal!" Akbar called out loudly. "You look just like a washerman's donkey with a load of clothes!"

Birbal quickly guessed the Emperor was trying to make a fool of him. So he retorted: "You're right, *Jahanpanah*. But I'm not carrying the load of one but three donkeys!"

Birbal's witty reply left Akbar speechless.

The Master Versus the Servant

The Court was faced with an unusual problem. Two men had come complaining that the other man was his servant! The servant had robbed his master years ago. And now he was pretending to be the master.

Akbar was unable to decide who was speaking the truth. So he called Birbal. The wise minister thought for a few minutes. "Aha!" Birbal exclaimed. "I have the solution."

Birbal then called the executioner. Both men were scared on seeing the executioner with his big axe! Birbal ordered the two men to lie down on the floor. They obeyed. "Keep your faces down!" Birbal barked.

They did so. "I'll now meditate for a few minutes. At the end of it, I'll know who's the servant pretending to be the master. The man who is lying will be beheaded immediately."

Birbal ordered the executioner to stand besides him. For the next few minutes, Birbal pretended to meditate. The executioner and Birbal were right behind the two men. Both couldn't see Birbal and the executioner. Suddenly, Birbal opened his eyes and exclaimed: "That man is the pretender! Behead him immediately!"

Suddenly, one of the two men jumped up in panic. "Please spare my life! I've wronged my master. I'm the servant. I'll never do such a thing ever again. But please spare my life."

Emperor Akbar spared his life. But the man was punished with a one-year jail term. The master had received justice within a day – only due to Birbal's clever trick.

Bangles and Stairs

'There must be some way to fool Birbal,' Akbar thought. Then an idea struck the Emperor. When he saw Birbal that morning, Akbar asked: "Birbal, can you tell me how many bangles your wife wears?"

Birbal replied: "No, Your Majesty, I can't."

"There!" said Akbar triumphantly. "You're not at all observant. How come you haven't noticed the number of bangles your wife uses? You see these everyday."

"*Jahanpanah*, bangles mean nothing to me. So I don't bother to count them. Besides, do you know the number of hair in your beard?" Birbal countered.

"Birbal, that's a silly comparison," Akbar said. "A person can't count his own hair. But your wife's bangles are bigger and fully visible to you."

Birbal quickly changed the topic. "Sire, let's go outside for some fresh air."

45

"So you admit defeat, don't you?" Akbar said gleefully, walking along with Birbal.

The cunning minister didn't reply as they walked down the palace steps towards the garden. As they went down the last stair, Birbal asked: "Your Majesty, do you know the number of steps down your palace stairs?"

Akbar didn't know what to say. "Why would I bother counting the palace steps?" Akbar asked.

"So you don't know the number of steps down the palace stairs. These steps are much bigger than my wife's bangles. Yet you expect me to know the number of my wife's bangles!" Birbal shot back, grinning wickedly.

The Emperor realised he'd made a fool of himself once more by challenging Birbal.

A Question of 'Like'

A miser (a person who spends very little money and simply collects it) led a miserable life in his hut. Whatever money he made, he saved. He spent very little on his food and clothing. Soon, he had saved a lot of gold coins. But he never used them. He kept all the gold in a pot.

One night, his hut caught fire. The miser managed to rush out. But he couldn't take his pot of gold along. And he didn't even have the guts to risk going inside. So he simply stood by moaning. He groaned that all his life's savings were going up in smoke.

A merchant was passing by. "Why cry for this miserable hut? You can always build a new one," he said.

"I'm not crying for the hut. I'm crying for the pot of gold left inside!" the miser disclosed.

"How much could your savings be?" the merchant inquired.

"Over 100 gold coins," the miser replied.

"I can risk my life and save your gold coins," the merchant offered. "But what will you give me in return?"

"I'll give you a gold coin!" the miser suggested.

"One miserable gold coin for saving 100 gold coins?" the merchant protested.

"Then take two," the miser was generous.

"No way! I'll only do it if you agree to let me decide. I'll then give you whatever I like. Is that agreed?"

This was not okay with the miser. But the poor man had no choice. His hut and savings were already going up in flames.

"Okay, okay. I'll let you decide," the miser agreed with great difficulty. So he told the merchant where his pot of gold was hidden.

The merchant rushed in and found the pot of gold. Grabbing it, he quickly dashed out. He then told the miser: "We agreed that I could give you whatever I liked. So I'm keeping all the gold and giving you the pot."

The miser protested loudly that this was cheating. Soon the miser and the merchant began fighting. They almost came to blows. Some passers-by separated the two. Both were taken to Court.

The merchant told Birbal that the miser had agreed to let him give whatever he liked. But the miser had now changed his mind.

Birbal asked the miser whether what the merchant said was true. The miser agreed it was true. "But I didn't expect to be cheated," the miser protested.

Birbal told the miser to stay calm. He then spoke to the merchant: "My dear man, you agreed to give this miser whatever you *liked*. Right?"

The merchant agreed this was true. So Birb .l asked: "And you *like* the gold coins, don't you?"

The merchant realised the trick question: "I do, but..."

"No ifs and buts!" Birbal replied. "Since you *like* the gold coins, you must give them to the miser! This is as per your own words."

The poor merchant was forced to follow Birbal's orders. Thus the miser was saved from being cheated. And the cunning merchant received nothing because he had tried to cheat the miser.

The Most-liked Profession

Which is the most-liked profession? This question entered Akbar's mind one day. So he asked his courtiers about this. The first one said business. The second said masonry. The third said carpentry. But one profession that got the most votes was the army.

Not convinced, the Emperor turned to Birbal. All eyes were on the wise minister. Birbal rose to his feet. "Your Majesty, the most popular profession is medicine."

All were surprised by this answer. So was Emperor Akbar. Why, the physicians in the city could be counted on one's fingertips. Strangely, even the Court physician was offended. "Birbal, you don't know how difficult it is to become a physician," he said.

The Emperor agreed. "Can you prove your statement, Birbal?" Akbar asked.

"Come with me tomorrow morning, Your Majesty. I'll then prove my statement," Birbal gave a sly smile.

Immediately, Akbar agreed. The next morning, Akbar went to meet Birbal in the marketplace. When he reached there, the Emperor was surprised. Birbal had a big bandage on his right hand.

"What happened, Birbal?" the Emperor asked, concerned.

"I cut my hand while slicing potatoes for breakfast," the wise minister replied.

"Birbal, you must wash that wound well. And don't forget to apply some turmeric. It will heal within two days," Akbar advised Birbal.

"I'll follow your advice, *Jahanpanah*," Birbal smiled. "But could you please do me a favour? Write down the names of all the physicians we meet today? I can't write with this bandaged hand."

"Of course, I will Birbal!" Akbar responded.

For the next few hours, the two of them sat on a charpoy in the marketplace. Every few minutes someone or the other would walk up to Birbal: "O Birbal, what's the matter?" On being told he'd cut his hand, each person gave some advice without being asked: "Why don't you use this... or that..."

And Akbar kept noting all the names of persons who advised Birbal. By afternoon, the list kept growing longer and longer. But there was no end to the people who kept giving unasked advice.

Finally, Akbar said: "Birbal, why don't we go home? People will keep advising you till evening!"

"Of course, Your Majesty! But first let me have a look at all these untrained physicians who gave me medical advice," Birbal grinned slyly.

Akbar handed the list over, suddenly realising something.

"*Jahanpanah*," Birbal exclaimed, "you forgot to put your name at the top of this list! You were the first person to give me medical advice."

Akbar smiled in defeat: "Birbal, you always prove your point by hook or by crook!"

51

What God Does...

Akbar once asked Birbal: "What does God do, Birbal?"
"Why, Sire," Birbal seemed surprised, "even a
shepherd boy could answer this question."

The Emperor was irritated by this response: "Oh,
would he? Then why don't you produce such a shepherd
boy before me?"

The next day, Birbal brought a young shepherd to
Court. The Emperor asked him: "What does God do,
young man?"

Unafraid, the village boy replied: "Is my Emperor
asking this question as a teacher or as a student?"

The Emperor was puzzled. "As a student," he replied.

"Then look at the student's cheekiness," the boy stated.
"The student continues sitting on the throne, while the
teacher stands before him!"

Akbar went red in the face. He quickly stood up and walked down. Leading the boy by the hand, he made him sit on the throne. Akbar took the shepherd's cloak and wrapped it around himself. With folded hands, he then asked the shepherd boy: "O teacher, could you please tell me what God does?"

The shepherd boy laughed: "God turns a shepherd boy into an Emperor! And an Emperor into a shepherd!"

Birbal looked at the Emperor. Akbar was speechless. Yes, God could do anything He pleased, the Emperor realised.

Which Came First?

During one of Akbar's durbars, a pandit visited the Court. He told the Emperor that he would like to ask him one question. But Akbar was very tired that day.

"Birbal, please answer panditji's question. I'm too tired to wait any longer," Akbar said.

"As you wish, Your Majesty," Birbal bowed.

The pandit then turned to Birbal: "You have a choice. I'll either ask one difficult question or a hundred easy ones."

Birbal looked at Akbar. It was clear that the Emperor would not sit for a hundred easy questions. "I'll answer one difficult question," Birbal replied.

"Fine!" said the pandit, flashing a cunning smile. "Which came first: the hen or the egg?"

"How silly!" Birbal responded. "The hen, of course!"

"What makes you so sure?" the pandit demanded.

"Now!" Birbal scolded him. "You had agreed to ask only one difficult question. I answered it! So why are you asking a second one?"

The Court and the Emperor roared with laughter at how Birbal tricked the pandit.

The Power of Chanting

Everyone knew of Birbal's wit and wisdom. But few knew that he was a devotee of Lord Rama. On one occasion, Akbar went hunting without his usual companions. He only took Birbal along.

After a long day's hunt, they failed to kill any animal. The Emperor and Birbal were both very hungry. So they halted at a forest clearing. Birbal squatted on the forest floor and closed his eyes.

A few minutes later, Akbar decided to go looking for some food. "Birbal, why don't you come along with me?" he suggested.

"You'll have to excuse me, Your Majesty," the minister replied. "I must continue chanting *Rama Nama Japam* (repeatedly saying Lord Rama's name)."

Akbar was offended at this direct refusal: "Simply chanting the name of your God will not get you any food!

56

You will have to go and look for it. Without any effort, you'll achieve nothing."

Birbal smiled: "Everything happens as per the Lord's will."

"That's what you think," the Emperor snapped at Birbal and walked away.

After walking for over a mile, Akbar felt tired. Then he noticed a house a hundred metres away. The Emperor was overjoyed. Surely he'd find food here. The people in the house were also delighted. The Emperor at their doorstep! They quickly offered Akbar all the food he could eat.

Akbar ate to his heart's content. Before leaving, he decided to take some food for Birbal. The owner of the house wrapped a plateful and gave it to the Emperor.

Half an hour later, Akbar reached Birbal. "Here!" the Emperor said. "I made the effort and got food. I also brought some for you. But by simply sitting here, what did you get?"

Birbal ignored the Emperor's taunt and simply ate the food quietly. When he had eaten, the Emperor repeated his unanswered question.

The wise Birbal smiled: "The power of *Rama Nama Japam* has just been revealed to me. Although you are the Emperor, today you had to beg for your food. And I was simply sitting here, chanting. Yet the Emperor himself went and got some food for me. So without any special effort, I received food. Thanks to the power of *Rama Nama Japam!*"

Yet again, the Emperor was too shocked to reply.

Sunshine and Shade

There was a strange problem in the Court. And Birbal couldn't solve it. Because he was the cause of the problem! It so happened that Akbar and Birbal had a quarrel. In anger, Birbal had walked out of the palace.

A few days later, Akbar began to feel the absence of his favourite minister. But no one in the Court knew how to find Birbal. Getting him back was the second problem. This was a problem Birbal would have solved soon. Yet, this was not possible. Since his disappearance was the first problem!

Akbar kept thinking of ways to get Birbal back. Suddenly, he found the answer one day. The Emperor announced a reward of 1,000 gold coins to any person who came to the palace while fulfilling a strange condition: the person must walk in the sun without an umbrella, but he should also be in the shade at the same time.

All the citizens wished they could win the 1,000 gold coins. But they knew the condition was impossible to fulfil.

One day, however, a villager came to Court. He told the Emperor that he had fulfilled his condition. So he must be given the prize. The Emperor asked him to prove his claim.

The man pointed to his charpoy: "Your Majesty, I held this string cot over my head while walking in the sun. But despite the sun, I was in the shade of the cot's strings!"

Indeed, this was a brilliant solution! But the Emperor was suspicious. Only one man could have thought of this solution. So Akbar called the villager to his side. "Tell me," the Emperor commanded, "who gave you this brilliant solution? Surely you did not think of this!"

"You are right, Your Majesty," the man revealed. "This is the idea of a man who's living with me."

Akbar was sure this man was Birbal. So he asked the villager to bring his guest to the Court immediately.

When the man presented himself in the Court, the Emperor was proved right. Akbar and Birbal embraced each other. They were happy on meeting again and quickly forgot their silly quarrel.

Story 24

Darkness Besides a Lamp

Early one morning, the Emperor and Birbal were enjoying the sunrise. Suddenly, they heard some noise nearby. They discovered that a group of travellers had been robbed. But the dacoits had already run away.

The Emperor sent his soldiers to chase them. However, the robbers had simply disappeared. Akbar was disappointed. So he told Birbal: "What's the use of being the Emperor of India if people can be robbed right before my eyes."

The ministers in Court gave various replies. But none satisfied the Emperor. Finally, Birbal told Akbar: "Sire, even the most powerful lamp that lights up the surroundings for miles still casts a dark shadow at its own feet."

The simplicity of this explanation convinced Akbar. He realised this was true. And he was consoled that crime in his kingdom could not be stopped totally.

The Purpose of Divine Intervention

Sometimes, Akbar purposely felt like arguing with Birbal. This was one such day. So the Badshah said: "Birbal, Hindus believe that Lord Vishnu one day heard the terrified cry of His elephant and rushed to help. But why would a God with so many servants Himself rush to help a servant?"

"Your Majesty," Birbal replied, "you will have the answer in a few days."

The Emperor agreed to wait.

Some days later, Birbal made a wax model of the Emperor's grandson. He also dressed him in the grandson's clothes.

The next morning, Birbal called one of the Emperor's servants. "Do as I tell you," Birbal said, "and you'll be richly rewarded. Take this doll near the pond where the Emperor will notice it. Then, pretend to fall and fling the doll into the pond. As you do so, utter a fear-stricken cry."

The man did just as Birbal told him. When the Emperor saw him fall and cry helplessly, Akbar quickly rushed there. The Emperor thought it was his grandson who had fallen into the pond. Without thinking, the Emperor jumped into the pond to save his grandson.

As Akbar struggled to save his 'grandson', Birbal stepped forward. "Why did Your Majesty rush in to save this doll when there are so many servants to do it?"

The Emperor didn't know what to say. He instantly realised he'd been tricked. Birbal then explained, "This is why Vishnu rushes to save anybody who seeks His help. In the Lord's eyes, all creatures are equally precious."

Unlucky Professions

Many courtiers were always plotting against Birbal. One day, a courtier asked: "Before you came to the Court, what was your profession?"

Birbal replied honestly: "I was a farmer."

"What about your father and grandfather?" the man asked.

"My father was a farmer. So was my grandfather, as well as my great-grandfather. For generations, our family has been farming," Birbal announced proudly.

The man questioned further: "How did all of them die?"

Again, Birbal was honest: "They all died in the field. My father died while harvesting the summer crop. My grandfather fell into our well in the field. My great-grandfather was struck by lightning while ploughing."

"Do you realise one thing?" the man asked. "Your family profession of farming is a very unlucky one."

Birbal looked the man straight in the face: "What's your family's profession?"

Replied the courtier: "Why, we have all been soldiers."

"Oh, I see," Birbal grinned. "How did your father die?"

"He died in the battlefield," the man answered proudly.

"What about your grandfather?" Birbal probed.

"Oh, he too died in the battlefield," the man hesitated.

"And your great-grandfather?" Birbal continued.

"He also died while fighting," the man replied slowly.

"There!" Birbal replied smugly. "So a soldier's profession is equally unlucky."

Then Birbal turned towards the Emperor and told the courtier: "Most of the Emperor's ancestors died in bed. So as per your logic, it's very dangerous to sleep in bed!"

The entire Court was drowned in laughter. But the courtier felt like drowning in shame!

Of Streets and Turns

The Persian Emperor had heard a lot about Akbar's wise minister, Birbal. So he decided to check whether these stories were true. For this, he sent his wisest minister to Hindustan.

The Persian minister reached the Mughal Court and was well received. A few days after arrival, he made his request. He wanted just one question answered: "How many turns are there in Agra's streets?"

The question took Akbar's ministers by surprise. Each and every minister simply scratched his head! Nobody had ever counted the number of turns in Agra's streets.

Badshah Akbar quickly sent Raja Mansingh to count the number of turns in Agra's streets! Raja Mansingh was told to complete the work in two days. He left immediately, since the task was very difficult.

That day, Birbal was unwell. So he arrived late in the Court. On entering, Birbal found Akbar and the other courtiers looking worried. Birbal enquired if there was something wrong.

Akbar told Birbal about the Persian Emperor's query. The Persian minister who had communicated the query was awaiting a response. Akbar also revealed that Raja Mansingh had been given two days' time to find out the answer.

Hearing this, Birbal was highly amused. "*Jahanpanah*, there was no need to send Raja Mansingh to count the turns in Agra's streets. The answer is very simple."

Everybody was surprised. They had been racking their brains for so many hours. But now Birbal claimed it was an easy question!

"If you know the answer, tell us immediately," Akbar commanded.

"Your Majesty, all the streets in the world have only two turns. A left turn and a right turn!" replied Birbal.

Everybody was amazed. This was a really simple answer! Why hadn't they thought of it?

The Persian minister was impressed by Birbal's prompt response. When he returned to Persia, he informed the Persian Emperor that Birbal was much wiser than his reputation!

Akbar's 'Greed'

For years, Akbar had one desire only: to outwit Birbal! Although he never succeeded, he didn't give up trying. When Akbar was blessed with a son, he held a grand feast. There an opportunity presented itself.

All courtiers and ministers had been invited for the feast. Even common men were allowed to attend the feast at a nearby ground. Food and wine flowed freely. People flocked to the place. Everybody agreed they hadn't seen such a grand feast.

Birbal was seated next to Akbar at the dinner feast. Countless dishes were being served. People feasted on whatever caught their fancy. There were vegetarian and non-vegetarian items. Along with the food, Akbar was also enjoying Birbal's stories.

After dinner, fruits were served. Akbar and Birbal were both eating a big bowl of dates. As they spoke, both kept throwing the seeds near their feet. Suddenly, Akbar had an idea. This was the perfect chance to have some fun. And to outsmart Birbal! Noticing the pile of date seeds near their feet, Akbar played a trick. He quietly pushed all his seeds on Birbal's side. Now Birbal's pile of seeds was huge. While Akbar had just a few date seeds near his feet.

A few seconds later, the Emperor looked down. He then pretended to be surprised. "Birbal, I never knew you were so greedy! How can you eat so many dates after having a hearty dinner?" Akbar asked loudly.

Guests in the hall fell silent. All eyes were focused on Birbal. What would he say? For the first time, it seemed Birbal would have no answer. Birbal calmly looked down. There was a huge pile of seeds near his feet. And there were almost none near Akbar's feet.

Birbal quickly knew Akbar had played a trick. But he was unconcerned. Coolly, he turned towards the Emperor. "You are right, Badshah. I've been very greedy, eating so many dates. However, at least I've only eaten the fruit and left the seeds. But you have eaten all the seeds also! Why, you have been twice as greedy!"

Akbar was very embarrassed. Once more, Birbal had had the last laugh. As for guests in the hall, none dared laugh openly!

The Crows in Agra

O n many occasions, people challenged Birbal. These
jealous persons wanted to prove that Birbal was not
really wise. But nobody succeeded.

A famous scholar once visited the Mughal Court.
"Birbal," the scholar challenged, "can you answer any
question I ask?"

"Only if you ask difficult ones!" Birbal quipped. The
entire Court laughed heartily.

The scholar was not amused: "Is that so? Then
answer this: How many crows live in Agra?"

"I'll let you know tomorrow morning!" Birbal told
him.

The scholar said he would return the next day for the
answer. Akbar was worried. "Birbal, no doubt you are

very clever. But even you cannot count all the crows in Agra," Akbar cautioned Birbal.

Birbal told the Emperor not to worry. "I'll give the answer tomorrow!" he insisted.

The next morning, the Court assembled. The scholar also presented himself. "Birbal, do you have the answer? Or do you accept defeat?" the man asked confidently.

"I have the answer, Sir," Birbal claimed. "Agra has 78,299 crows!"

The scholar protested: "How can you be sure?"

"I have counted all the crows personally!" Birbal replied. "If you have any doubts, count them yourself!"

The scholar knew Birbal was bluffing. So he tried to corner him. "Suppose there are more crows than that?" the man inquired.

"Then it means that crows from other cities are visiting their relatives!" Birbal revealed.

"And suppose the number is lesser than what you claim?" the man continued.

"That can only mean crows from Agra are out of town visiting their relatives!" Birbal shot back.

Within seconds, the Court echoed with the sound of laughter. The scholar realised Birbal had a ready answer to every question. He was forced to admit defeat.

The Mendicant's Queries

Emperor Akbar once faced a strange problem. Many passers-by, especially mendicants (sadhus), would seek shelter in the cool surroundings of the palace. So the Emperor passed an order: no one should take shelter near the palace walls.

Many people hated this order, including the mendicants. But they were forced to obey it. Soon, this order made Akbar very unpopular. Birbal knew the unjust order was giving a just man like Akbar a bad name. So he decided to do something.

Early one morning, the royal guards found a mendicant leaning against the palace wall. The guards tried to drive him away. But the man refused to leave. He was also not bothered about threats of being jailed. Since Akbar did not like holy men being harassed, the guards were helpless.

Some time later, the Emperor returned from his morning walk. He noticed the mendicant leaning against the palace wall. The royal guards were simply standing nearby, doing nothing. Akbar was furious. Why was his order not being followed? He questioned the guards. They told the Emperor that the mendicant simply refused to go away.

So the Emperor confronted the man himself. "What do you think you're doing? Don't you know people can't stand here?" the Emperor demanded.

The mendicant looked at Akbar without answering. This made Akbar furious. "How dare you ignore my question!" Akbar shouted. "Why don't you go away?"

"I will, if you answer a few questions," the mendicant replied cheekily.

"What do you mean?" the Emperor glared.

"Just what I said!" the man replied, unafraid.

"What do you wish to know?" the Emperor asked.

"Who lived here before you?" the mendicant asked.

"My father, Emperor Humayun, of course!" Akbar said.

"Before him?" the man continued.

"My grandfather, Emperor Babar!" Akbar responded.

"And before him?" the mendicant went on.

"The Lodi king, Ibrahim Lodi, whom my grandfather defeated in battle," Akbar was losing patience.

"It seems many persons had occupied the palace before you," the mendicant said. "So what makes you think this is your exclusive property?"

"How dare you!" the Emperor screamed.

"Why not?" the man coolly replied. "With so many people living here, this is like a *dharamshala*! Everyone lives here for a short while and then moves on. Only to be replaced by another person."

Akbar slowly realised the man was speaking the truth. "Even this earth is like an inn or *dharamshala*. We all come here for a short stay. Then we depart for our final abode. We are just temporary occupants. This world is just a short journey. So why prevent others from enjoying the journey, any place, any time?" the mendicant demanded.

"You are right, holy man. I am pleased by your wisdom and courage," the Emperor patted the man. The moment the Emperor went close, he was surprised.

This was no mendicant! "Birbal, it's you! I should have known only one man could have spoken like that," the Emperor exclaimed.

That very day, Emperor Akbar cancelled his unjust order. And everyone thanked Birbal for making the Emperor change his mind.

The Emperor's Land

Sometimes, Akbar would get angry with people. Then, nothing could save them – except Birbal. This was one such occasion. Some eunuchs (*hijras*) were performing before the Emperor. Without thinking, one eunuch uttered a bad word during their play. The Emperor was very offended. He immediately ordered every eunuch to leave the kingdom. Eunuchs who ignored the order would be hanged, the Emperor ruled.

All the eunuchs were terrified. If they disobeyed, they'd be killed. But if they obeyed, how would they survive in a strange land? Strangers were never welcomed elsewhere. And definitely not eunuchs!

The eunuchs knew death would meet them everywhere. So they acted sensibly. The eunuchs rushed to Birbal! "*Huzoor*, only you can help us!" the eunuchs pleaded with folded hands. "It was only a play we were performing before the Emperor. One bad word should not be a reason to destroy all of us."

Birbal listened to them patiently. He thought for a few minutes. Then he told them not to worry. There was a way out...

The next day, Akbar was preparing for a hunt. So he went into the garden to fetch his horse. As he mounted his horse, Akbar looked up. Suddenly, his mouth opened in surprise. All the trees were filled with people!

"What's going on here?" the Emperor roared.

A soldier replied: "Sire, these are all eunuchs! They have taken shelter in the trees."

"Eunuchs!" the Emperor was very angry. "I ordered them to leave the Empire. Why are they still here? They should be put to death!"

Immediately, the chief of the eunuchs approached Akbar. "Forgive us, Your Majesty!"

"I ordered all eunuchs to leave my Empire. Why didn't you leave? I'll have all of you beheaded!" Akbar warned.

"Forgive us, Sire!" the chief eunuch said. "We tried our best to leave your kingdom. But Your Majesty rules entire Hindustan and almost the whole world. So where could we go? It is only to follow your orders that we climbed these trees! In this way, we are away from the land you rule over!"

The Emperor's anger slowly faded. He was pleased with this clever response. "I'll pardon each one of you," Akbar promised, "if you tell me who suggested this clever answer."

"Birbal helped us, Your Majesty!" the eunuchs replied together.

"I knew it!" the Emperor nodded. Thereafter, all the eunuchs were forgiven.

The 'No!' Approach

Birbal never had to look for enemies. They always queued up seeking revenge! An ambitious courtier was one such man. This courtier wanted to make his son the royal treasurer. He tried very hard for this. But he never succeeded. The courtier thought Birbal was spoiling his chances. So he decided to take revenge.

He received a chance when Birbal once came to the Court late. That day, the courtier told the Emperor: "Sire, Birbal takes the Court for granted. He thinks it's his *jagir*. He must be taught a lesson."

Akbar pretended to agree: "What do you suggest I do?"

"You must deny every request he makes today," the courtier suggested.

"Done!" the Emperor promised.

When Birbal came after noon, Akbar asked: "Birbal, why are you so late?"

Birbal: "Your Majesty, my wife is unwell. Please forgive me for being late."

Akbar: "I will not!"

Birbal: "Shall we then discuss matters of the Court?"

Akbar: "No, we will not!"

Birbal: "Then can I go home?"

Akbar: "No, you will stay till evening!"

Birbal: "May I sit down at least?"

Akbar: "No! You must keep standing!"

The Emperor's angry replies and voice told Birbal something was wrong. He looked around the Court. Seeing Birbal's discomfort, the courtier couldn't stop grinning. Birbal immediately guessed who had poisoned Akbar's mind. So he decided to teach the troublemaker a severe lesson.

Birbal: "Sire, I have one final request. Please appoint this courtier's son as the royal treasurer."

Akbar: "No! I will not and never will!"

Before the courtier knew what was happening, Birbal had played the courtier's own trick on him. From that day onwards, other jealous courtiers feared opposing Birbal.

The Egg Trick

Try as he might, Akbar could never fool Birbal. But now he had a "foolproof" plan. The wise minister was coming late to the Court that day. So before Birbal reached the Court, Akbar gave each of his ministers an egg. And he told them what they had to do.

When Birbal arrived, Akbar put his plan into action. "I had a dream last night," the Emperor told the Court. "I dreamt that if each minister fetched an egg from the royal pond, it would prove their honesty."

The Emperor asked each minister to visit the pond one by one. After a while, each returned with an egg. Of course, the Emperor had already told them to hide their eggs near the pond.

Finally, it was Birbal's turn. But he had not been given any egg. So when he reached the pond, he didn't find any egg. Birbal searched awhile. Soon, he gave up. But his suspicions were aroused. How did each minister return with an egg? There was only one way... Birbal understood this was Akbar's trick. But he was not bothered. He simply returned to the Court empty-handed.

When Birbal entered the Court, everyone watched him closely. Suddenly, Birbal began to crow like a cock! The courtiers wondered if he'd gone mad. "Birbal, where's your egg?" Akbar inquired.

In reply, Birbal crowed again! "Birbal, what's wrong with you?" Akbar demanded. "Where's your egg?"

Birbal crowed like a cock once again. Then he replied: "*Jahanpanah*, until now you saw only the hens. Naturally, they produced their eggs. What you see now is the only cock in the Mughal Court. Being a cock, how can I lay eggs?"

The Court was consumed in fits of laughter. Akbar was also forced to laugh. "Birbal, you're simply too smart to be fooled!" the Emperor complimented him.

How to Retrieve a Ring

Akbar once decided to check if any minister was as wise as Birbal. So he gave a test to all of them. But Birbal was not asked to participate.

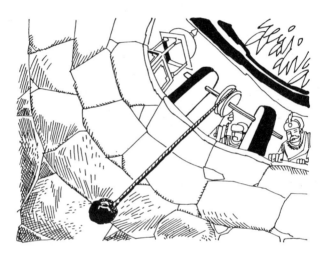

In the presence of the ministers, the Emperor flung his ring into a dry well. "Now," said Akbar, "without entering the well, the ring must be recovered."

The ministers tried all sorts of tricks. But they simply couldn't get the ring out. A magnet tied to a string was let down. But the gold ring was not attracted to the magnet. An arrow with a rope tied to it was shot at the ring. But this too didn't work.

At the end of an hour, the ministers admitted defeat. Finally, Birbal spoke: "*Jahanpanah*, can I now try my luck?"

"There's no other option!" Akbar replied.

As everyone watched, Birbal picked some fresh cow dung. Taking careful aim, he threw it on top of the ring. He then tied a stone to a long string. This he flung on the soft cow dung. The other end of the string was in his hand. This end he now tied to the pulley of the well.

"Your Majesty, before sunset you'll have your ring back," Birbal promised. Everyone returned to the Court.

In the evening, everybody reassembled near the well. Birbal took the string from the pulley of the well. He tugged on it. The cow dung in the well had hardened. He quickly pulled the string up. On the other end, the cow dung rose with the string. In the centre of the dry cow dung was the Emperor's shining gold ring.

For the hundredth time, what was difficult for others was child's play for Birbal. In appreciation, the Emperor said: "Birbal, you may keep this ring as a gift from me. It's a tribute to your wit and wisdom."

Greater Than God

Two wandering poets from a faraway kingdom once arrived at the Mughal Court. They recited songs, poems and hymns. Hearing the recital, everyone was delighted. So was Emperor Akbar. Pleased, the Emperor rewarded them with gold coins and other riches. Both poets were very thankful. They had never seen so much gold before.

To express gratitude, the poets sang in praise of Emperor Akbar. They said Akbar was learned and wise. He was brave and just. One of the poets then got carried away. Akbar was the greatest king to ever rule this earth, the poet said. He was even "greater than God"!

Having said these words, the poet bowed. Taking hold of their belongings, both poets left the Court. As the Court thought about the second poet's words, the courtiers were silent. How could the poet compare a human being to God? Although Akbar was a great Emperor, how could he be greater than God? These thoughts passed through everyone's minds. But no one dared say so before the Badshah.

Emperor Akbar looked around the Court. He realised why everyone was silent. So he decided to have some fun! "It seems I'm now greater than God!" Akbar pretended to be serious.

All the ministers looked at one another. Had the Emperor really believed the poet's words? Had power gone to his head?

Again, Emperor Akbar looked at his courtiers. It was obvious he expected a response. Fearfully, the courtiers agreed that... "Akbar was the greatest". Indeed, he was "even greater than God"!

Akbar kept looking all around the Court. He hoped someone would have the courage to speak the truth. But everyone agreed: "Akbar was greater than God"!

The Emperor was disappointed. He began to feel irritated. "So there's nobody who feels I'm not greater than God?" Akbar asked. One by one, every courtier insisted that he was greater than God.

Perhaps Birbal would speak the truth, the Emperor felt. So he turned towards Birbal. "What do you think Birbal? Who's greater – God or Emperor Akbar?" the Badshah demanded.

"There's no doubt," Birbal replied, "that you are greater than God!"

The entire Court was shocked. All the courtiers held their breath. The Emperor wondered: 'Is Birbal trying to make a fool of me?'

"Are you joking, Birbal?" the Emperor demanded. "If so, this is not a topic to joke about."

"Not at all, Your Majesty," Birbal insisted. "I wouldn't lie to you."

"Can you prove your statement?" Akbar asked.

"I can, Sire," Birbal said. "You are greater than God because you can do something even God cannot."

"What would that be?" the Emperor asked. He still doubted Birbal's intentions.

"Your Majesty, if anyone displeases you, he can be exiled or banished from your kingdom. But God cannot do this. If a person displeases God, he cannot be banished from God's kingdom. God rules the entire earth and the heavens. There's no place in the universe where God does not rule. So He cannot banish anyone from His kingdom. But you can always do so. In this respect, you are surely greater than God!"

"Birbal, you are unbelievable!" the Emperor exclaimed. Slowly, every man in the Court rose to his feet. Within seconds, the entire Court was clapping. Truly, Birbal's wisdom was unmatched.

Akbar's Strange Request

It was a cold winter morning. Akbar woke up earlier than usual. Sleepily, he rubbed his fingers against his unshaved beard. He then called out: "Is anyone around? Quick! Call him at once!"

The guard standing outside the Emperor's door was confused. Whom did the Emperor seek? How was he supposed to know? Without knowing, how could the guard call "him"? But if the guard didn't follow orders, he'd be in real trouble.

So he went to another guard. The other man was equally confused. What could the Emperor have meant by: "Call him at once!"

The first guard then spoke to another guard. He too was of no help. So yet another guard was asked. This man too couldn't guess what Akbar meant. Soon, all the guards knew the Emperor had summoned someone. But no one knew who was called. There was total confusion.

Frightened, the first guard rushed to Birbal. He had to save his job. Birbal calmed the man down. He then asked him to explain the exact situation. The man repeated what had happened. Then Birbal inquired about the Emperor's exact words. The guard said: "The Emperor didn't ask for anyone specifically. He simply told me: 'Call him at once!' *Huzoor*, how am I supposed to know whom to call? Please help me. Or I'll lose my job."

Birbal thought about the situation. Even he was unable to understand what the Emperor meant. "Tell me," Birbal told the guard, "what exactly was the Emperor doing when he made this request?"

"Nothing, Sir. He was just getting out of bed. He simply rubbed his unshaved chin. Then he spoke to me immediately," the man revealed.

"Aha!" smiled Birbal. "I know what the Emperor meant. Take the barber to the Emperor at once. That will solve the problem."

The guard did as told. He presented himself before Akbar along with the barber. Now, the Emperor was puzzled. He wondered: 'When I didn't mention any name, how did the guard know I wanted the barber?'

"Tell me," Akbar asked the guard, "how did you know I wanted the barber?"

"Your Majesty, I didn't! It was Birbal who guessed you wanted the barber," the guard revealed.

Akbar was not surprised to hear who had solved the problem. For Birbal, nothing was impossible.

The Toilet Portrait

Very few rulers were strong enough to fight Akbar. One ruler who gave Akbar a tough time was Maharana Pratap Singh. This brave ruler and his army fought many battles with the Mughals. Unable to defeat Maharana Pratap, Akbar felt frustrated. In anger, Akbar hung a portrait of Maharana Pratap in his toilet.

One day, Birbal noticed Maharana Pratap's portrait in Akbar's toilet. This was very offensive to Birbal. He was shocked by Akbar's mean act. The Emperor must be taught a lesson, Birbal decided.

That evening, when Akbar was resting, Birbal suddenly entered and felt his pulse. "Is Your Majesty feeling better now?" Birbal inquired.

Akbar was puzzled: "What's wrong? I'm absolutely fine!"

"Are you?" Birbal pretended to be surprised. "I thought you were unwell. Just this morning I saw Maharana Pratap's portrait in your toilet."

"So?" Akbar wondered.

"I concluded that you're probably suffering from constipation and couldn't pass motions! I thought seeing Maharana Pratap's portrait helped you clear your bowels immediately. Fear usually does that, Your Majesty," Birbal said seriously.

Akbar quickly realised what Birbal meant. He immediately removed Maharana Pratap's portrait from the toilet.

New Moon Versus Full Moon

Birbal and Abul Fazl (another of Akbar's nine jewels) once visited Persia. On reaching there, they presented themselves before the Persian Emperor. While paying their respects, Abul Fazl simply bowed.

But Birbal bowed and went further. He said the Persian Emperor's reign was like the glory of the full moon. Pleased, the Persian Emperor inquired how he would describe Akbar's reign. Birbal replied that Akbar's reign was like the new moon.

Abul Fazl was shocked. How could Birbal say Akbar was only like the new moon? And he compared the Persian Emperor to the full moon! This was an insult to the Mughal Emperor.

Abul Fazl didn't say anything to Birbal in Persia. But the moment they returned to India, Fazl opened his mouth.

He told Emperor Akbar exactly what Birbal had said in the Persian Court.

Naturally, Akbar was furious. How dare his own minister compare him to the small new moon? Akbar summoned his offending minister. "Birbal, did you say the Persian Emperor was the full moon, while I was only like the new moon?"

"Of course, Your Majesty! That's exactly what I said," smiled Birbal.

Akbar, Abul Fazl and all the other ministers were surprised. Perhaps Birbal had lost his mind. "Birbal," Akbar spoke angrily, "are you saying I'm inferior to the Persian Emperor?"

"God forbid, *Jahanpanah*!" Birbal exclaimed. "How could I even think such a thing? Leave alone say it!"

"Then what did you mean by your unfair comparison," Akbar demanded.

"Your Majesty, my words have been misunderstood," Birbal explained. "The full moon is the last stage of the moon's growth. It has no scope for advancement. Thereafter, it only declines. That's the position of the Persian Empire. However, you are like the new moon. Your Empire is at the start of a phenomenal growth, just like the new moon. The Mughal Empire is destined to grow to its full potential. Yet, at the highest point of its growth the Persian Empire is still small compared to your Empire, which is larger even in its first stage. Now, you can judge whether my words were a compliment or an insult."

Everybody finally realised the clever comparison Birbal had made. Even the Persian Emperor had failed to understand the real point. Abul Fazl felt foolish. Birbal had once again added to his immense reputation. Just like the new moon, Birbal's reputation grew everyday.

How to Divide Friends

When Birbal was absent, Akbar realised his true value. Once, Birbal had gone visiting his relatives. During this time, Akbar was worried about his 16-year-old son, Prince Salim (later famous as Emperor Jehangir). The Prince had a good-for-nothing friend, Yusuf. In Yusuf's company, Prince Salim had picked up many bad habits.

Worried, Akbar consulted his ministers. There were various suggestions. "Send Prince Salim elsewhere for some time." "Banish Yusuf from the kingdom." "Don't allow the two to meet again." "The Prince must be told his friend is bad." Although the suggestions were many, none seemed practical.

The day Birbal returned, Akbar told him about his worry. Birbal thought it over. He then replied: "Your Majesty, give me two days' time. Your problem will be solved."

The very next day, Birbal met Yusuf. Salim also happened to be present. Birbal quietly took Yusuf aside. Prince Salim noticed this. The cunning Birbal then whispered in Yusuf's ear: "Yusuf, the sun always rises in the east."

Then Birbal moved away and said loudly: "Don't disclose this to anyone." Having said this, Birbal went away.

Within seconds, Prince Salim walked over to Yusuf. "What did Birbal whisper in your ear?" the Prince demanded.

"Oh, nothing at all!" Yusuf said. This was true, because Yusuf had not understood what Birbal said!

But Prince Salim was suspicious. "You're lying! Birbal whispered something," the Prince insisted.

"Actually, I couldn't understand what he said," Yusuf replied.

"I thought you were my friend. But you can only be my friend if you tell me what Birbal said," the Prince threatened.

"He spoke some rubbish: 'The sun always rises in the east', or something like that. He really did," Yusuf swore.

"You are a dirty liar!" the Prince shouted. "I'll never talk to you again."

"And you're a bloody fool!" Yusuf shouted back. "Because you don't believe the truth. I will also never talk to you since you don't trust me."

Hiding behind a tree, Birbal watched the drama. The Emperor would be pleased with what he had achieved. Indeed, Yusuf and Prince Salim never spoke to each other again. And the Emperor rewarded Birbal handsomely for separating the two friends so easily.

The Sighted Blind

The Empress was always giving charity. Now, she wished to donate money to blind people. Akbar ordered a survey to find out the number of blind persons in his kingdom. The day the details came in, Akbar told Birbal: "There are very few blind people in our kingdom. This is good."

"Your Majesty, there are more blind people than you think!" Birbal commented.

"How can you say so?" the Emperor demanded.

"Your Majesty, there are many who have eyes but are still blind," Birbal revealed.

"Birbal, you're talking rubbish!" Akbar insisted. "Can you show me even one person like that?"

"Of course! I'll show you many!" Birbal accepted the challenge.

Some days later, Birbal began stringing a charpoy in the centre of the marketplace! An assistant stood by, taking notes.

Throughout the day, people walked up to Birbal. "What are you doing, Birbal?" "What's going on, Birbal?" "What are you up to, Birbal?" The questions ran along the same lines. Each time, the assistant noted the questioner's name.

By afternoon, the news had reached Akbar. The Emperor rushed over to check what was up. "Birbal, what are you doing here?" the Emperor asked.

Birbal ignored the Emperor. Turning to his assistant, he said: "Take down the Emperor's name."

"Birbal, you haven't answered my question!" the Emperor said impatiently. "What are you up to?"

"*Jahanpanah*," Birbal said gleefully, "a few days ago I told you there were people who had eyes but were still blind. Today, I'm noting the names of all these blind people. Despite seeing that I'm stringing a charpoy, they keep asking what I'm doing!"

The Emperor suddenly realised that Birbal had fooled him – yet again!

Money Versus Justice

The Emperor once decided to check his ministers' likes and dislikes. So he asked: "Between justice and a gold coin, what would each person choose?"

Without exception, everyone claimed they'd opt for justice. Birbal kept silent. "Birbal, you haven't replied. What would you choose?" the Emperor asked.

"The gold coin, obviously!" Birbal replied.

The entire Court was shocked by his reply. But the courtiers were secretly pleased. No one had ever managed to make a fool of Birbal. Now he was doing this himself!

Even Emperor Akbar was surprised by the reply. "Birbal, I'm shocked! How can you be so greedy and choose a gold coin over justice? Even my servants would prefer justice over money," the Emperor scolded him.

"It's all very simple, Your Majesty," Birbal reasoned. "Why should one seek what he has? You have ensured justice for every man in the kingdom. I've always received justice in every way. So I don't need justice at all. However, due to heavy family expenses I'm always short of money. So I have chosen the gold coin."

The Emperor was very pleased with Birbal's thoughtful response. He immediately gifted him one thousand gold coins.

The Begum's Most Precious Possession

There were moments when Akbar did things in anger. Then he would pass orders that he later felt sorry about. Once, the Emperor was very upset with one of his wives. "Begum, I never want to see your face again!" the Emperor shouted.

The frightened begum was forced to rush away from his presence. She was confused and helpless. 'What will I do? Where will I go?' she wondered.

Then she thought of Birbal. This is what everybody in trouble did – think of God... or Birbal! He was the only human who could save her. The begum rushed over to the wise minister's house. She told him exactly what had happened.

Birbal calmed her down. He then explained: "Such quarrels, Begum Sahiba, are part of married life. Don't worry. Do as I tell you and the Emperor will soon forgive you."

He then told the begum exactly what was to be done. Having listened to Birbal, she returned to the palace. Presenting herself before Akbar, she said: "I had decided to serve you all my life. But since you wish me to leave, I will do just that.

The Emperor was really furious. "Why have you come in my presence? Say what you must and leave immediately!" the Badshah commanded.

"My Lord, since I'll never ever see you again, I've a request. Please come to my palace for dinner tonight. I will then leave your kingdom. But you must also grant me one last wish. I will take along with me my most precious possession. This will leave me with fond memories of Your Highness," the begum said.

The Emperor didn't wish to have dinner with the begum. But he agreed to her request. Perhaps he would then get rid of her forever. Happy that he had agreed, the begum left.

That night, Akbar visited the begum's palace for dinner. All the Emperor's favourite dishes had been prepared. After the meal, the begum offered Akbar a glass of warm milk. Unknown to Akbar, she had mixed sleeping pills in the milk. The Emperor became unconscious after drinking the milk and fell onto the bed. Quickly, the begum called Birbal.

Within minutes, Birbal came with a carriage. Attendants hurriedly placed Akbar into the carriage. The doors were then closed and the carriage sped away. The begum too was seated inside. Twenty minutes later, the begum halted the carriage outside her father's house.

The next morning, Akbar awoke with a heavy head. He looked around, puzzled. "Where am I?" he asked aloud.

The begum was seated beside his bed. "My Lord, y u are at my father's place," she said softly.

"How dare you bring me here!" Akbar screamed.

"But my Lord, you agreed I could take my most precious possession along. Naturally, I couldn't leave you behind! That's why I brought you here," the begum explained tearfully.

Akbar quickly realised the trick his begum had played. He also knew only one person could have advised this course of action. "Begum," Akbar laughed, "so you sought Birbal's advice, didn't you?"

The begum's toothy smile told Akbar what he already knew. The Emperor forgave his begum. That very day, both returned to their palace.

Stone Flowers Versus Real Ones

The Emperor was fond of strolling in the royal gardens every evening. Birbal accompanied him on many occasions. One day, Akbar said: "What a beautiful flower! No man could ever make something so beautiful."

"I beg your pardon, Your Majesty," Birbal said. "But there are times when man can produce something more beautiful."

"Birbal, you are almost always right," the Emperor admitted. "But I disagree with you now. There's no way man can make something more beautiful."

Birbal kept silent, as he did on many occasions. Sooner or later, an opportunity presented itself and Birbal proved his point.

A week later, Birbal led an expert craftsman into the Emperor's presence. The man had made an intricate stone carving of a bouquet of flowers. Akbar was impressed by the exquisite work. He quickly rewarded the man with a thousand gold coins.

A few minutes later, a small boy entered the Court. He held a bouquet of beautiful, fresh and fragrant flowers. Bowing, he presented the bouquet to the Emperor. Akbar quickly accepted it, sniffed the flowers and kept them aside. He rewarded the boy with a gold coin for his fresh bouquet.

"Well, well, Your Majesty," Birbal commented. "It seems that the stone carving was more beautiful than the real thing. The stone flowers fetched a thousand gold coins. But the real thing only got one gold coin!"

Akbar didn't know what to say. Time and again, Birbal kept outwitting him.

The Art of Cooking *Khichdi*

It was a freezing winter day. Akbar and Birbal were strolling along the banks of a lake. Suddenly, Birbal commented aloud: "Man will do anything for money!"

The Emperor thought about this. An idea then occurred to him. Here was a real chance to disprove Birbal. The Emperor walked to the water's edge. He dipped his finger into the lake. The water was freezing cold.

"I don't agree, Birbal," Akbar said. "For example, no man would spend an entire night in the cold water of this lake."

"Not at all!" Birbal differed. "I could find someone, *Jahanpanah.*"

"If you can find one man, Birbal," the Emperor challenged, "I'll award him one thousand gold coins!"

102

Birbal accepted the challenge. For the next few days, Birbal spoke to many people. No one wanted to risk spending a night in freezing water. Luckily, Birbal met a poor man. He was willing to spend an entire night in the lake's cold water. One thousand gold coins was something he could never even imagine. For this, he'd take any risk.

On the appointed night, the poor man entered the cold water. The Emperor posted some guards to make sure he didn't cheat.

The next morning, the poor man was produced before Akbar. He was shivering very badly.

"Did you spend the whole night in the cold water?" the Emperor demanded.

"I did, Your Highness," the poor man shivered as he spoke.

"How did you manage such a difficult task?" the Emperor asked.

"I did not think about the cold, Your Highness," the poor man revealed. "There was a street light nearby. So, throughout the dark night, I kept my attention on this light."

"What? You kept looking at a warm street lamp? In that case, there will be no reward," Akbar announced. "Because you broke the rules. You stayed in the cold water thanks to the warmth of the street lamp!"

The man protested that this was not true. But Emperor Akbar did not change his decision. There would be no reward of one thousand gold coins. Feeling cheated, the poor man met Birbal. He explained how he was not given the reward although he had spent the entire night in the lake. Birbal told the man to leave the matter to him. He should simply go home. His problem would be solved soon.

The next day, Birbal did not attend Court. Akbar waited a few hours. Then he sent his guards to meet Birbal. The guards went and spoke to Birbal.

An hour later, they returned with a strange tale. Birbal, the guards said, could not attend the Court because he was busy preparing *khichdi*! He could only come after his *khichdi* was cooked. The Emperor found this excuse strange. But he didn't say anything.

A few hours later, there was still no sign of Birbal. So the Emperor himself went over to investigate. On entering Birbal's house, Akbar was amazed. Birbal was sitting before a pot placed over an open fire. However, the pot was at least six feet above the flame! Birbal sat patiently waiting for the *khichdi* to cook!

Akbar and his attendants burst into uncontrolled laughter. "Birbal," Akbar demanded, "you really think the fire can cook *khichdi* placed six feet above it?"

"Why not?" Birbal replied calmly.

"That's impossible!" Akbar shot back.

"Not at all! It's possible. Just like how the poor man received heat from a street lamp that was over 100 metres away from the freezing water!"

The Emperor immediately realised his mistake. He had been unjust in not giving the poor man his reward. The very next day, the poor man was summoned. He was given the thousand gold coins along with some other gifts.

Tale of the Mango Tree

Ramu and Shamu were quarrelsome neighbours. They always spent their time fighting. But now things had gone too far. Therefore, the two were forced to approach Birbal. Both claimed they owned a mango tree that stood outside their house.

Birbal questioned them in detail. However, no positive conclusion could be drawn. It seemed the mango tree was in no-man's land. So Birbal told them to go home and return the next day. He would find some way to solve the problem.

The minute they left, Birbal called his servant. He instructed the man to follow both men. When they had entered their homes, the servant was to wait for a few minutes. Then he should shout, "Some thieves are stealing mangoes from the tree!" He would then report the reactions of both Ramu and Shamu.

The servant quickly followed both men. An hour later, he returned. He had done as told. On hearing that thieves were stealing mangoes from the tree, Ramu and Shamu both reacted in different ways.

Shamu said: "I'm busy right now. I'll see to it later."

Ramu rushed out with a stick, shouting: "Who's stealing mangoes from my tree? I'll thrash him black and blue!"

Birbal found this fact interesting. He told the servant to keep quiet about this discovery.

The next day, Ramu and Shamu presented themselves before Birbal. The wise minister told them: "Neither of you admits you are not the real owner. So I'm left with no choice but to cut down the mango tree. The wood will then be divided between the two of you."

Shamu immediately agreed. "This is the only way out!" he said.

Ramu was horrified! "*Huzoor*, the mango tree is like my own baby. I've looked after it since childhood. How can I agree to this decision? You're most welcome to give the entire tree to Shamu. I don't mind. But please don't cut it down. I shall never make a claim on it."

Finally, there were no doubts whatsoever about the tree's real owner. Birbal announced that now onwards the tree belonged officially to Ramu. As for Shamu, he received what he deserved – one month in prison for lying and cheating.

Giving and Receiving

There were rare occasions when Akbar asked unusual questions. Naturally, nobody could answer them. That is, nobody except Birbal. This was one such day. The Emperor asked a crowded Court: "I have observed a strange thing. When someone gives another person something, the giver's hand is always above the receiver's hand. Is there any instance when the giver's hand is below and the receiver's above?"

People thought and thought. But no one could think of a single exception. After a while, the Emperor turned to Birbal, as he always did! "Is there any exception, Birbal?" Akbar asked.

"No, Your Majesty, there is none!" almost everybody chorused in unison.

"I don't agree," Birbal replied. "There is always an exception to every rule. Here too, there is one. When you offer someone snuff! In this case, the receiver's hand is always above the person giving the snuff. That is the only way the receiver can pick up the snuff."

"You are great, Birbal!" Akbar exclaimed.

The Court had no option but to agree.

A Horse and Two 'Owners'

The legend of Akbar and his Nine Jewels-had spread far and wide. Chandra Varma, the King of Tripura, had heard many tales about Akbar and Birbal. So he decided to travel to the Mughal Court for a first-hand experience.

King Chandra Varma mounted his best horse for the long journey. After he had ridden a hundred miles or so, he saw a man limping on the road. A kind man, Chandra Varma stopped his horse. "Where are you going?" he asked the man.

"I am going to Agra," the man replied.

"How fortunate! I too am headed for Agra. You're welcome to travel with me," Chandra Varma offered.

The man quickly accepted. On the way, he revealed that his name was Vishnu Sharma. For the next few days,

Chandra Varma and Vishnu Sharma exchanged stories about themselves. However, Chandra Varma did not reveal his true identity.

Many days later, they reached Agra. "Okay, my friend, I shall now drop you off here," Chandra Varma told Sharma.

"What do you mean?" Vishnu Sharma demanded. "You get off here!"

Chandra Varma was shocked. Soon, a quarrel began. Varma and Sharma almost came to blows. By now, a large crowd had collected. People were confused. Each man claimed the horse was his and the other person was a liar!

"Let's take both to Birbal," a man in the crowd suggested.

An hour later, Varma and Sharma were produced in the Court. The horse was present too! Birbal heard both parties. He then told both of them to go away for the day. They were to return to the Court the next morning. "The horse, however, will stay with me," Birbal said.

Both men agreed. There was no choice, anyway! The moment the two stepped out, Birbal asked an attendant to take charge of the horse. He was to release the horse outside the Court and watch whom the animal followed – Varma or Sharma. He was then to come back with the horse.

The attendant left immediately with the horse. Half an hour later, he returned. The man reported that the horse had followed Chandra Varma. Birbal thanked the attendant and told him to rope the horse in the stable.

The next morning, Varma and Sharma presented themselves in the Court. Both men exchanged dirty looks. Birbal seemed highly amused. "Okay," Birbal said, "both of you can claim your horse from the stable. Sharma, you go first."

Sharma left quickly for the stable. The attendant followed him. As Sharma neared the stable, he slowed down. Inside the stable, Sharma was confused. All the horses looked the same to him! After spending over five minutes, he still couldn't decide which horse was his!

He was forced to return to the Court empty-handed.

"Varma, you may now go and claim your horse," Birbal said.

Again, the attendant quickly followed Varma. The horse neighed with joy the moment Chandra Varma entered the stable. The animal walked towards Varma and licked his hand. The attendant then led man and animal to the Court.

In the Court, Chandra Varma revealed his real identity. He was none other than the King of Tripura. So Akbar greeted him warmly with the respect due to a king. The horse naturally stayed with Chandra Varma. And Akbar ordered that Vishnu Sharma be given 100 lashes. This was followed by a three-month jail term.

Thus Chandra Varma, the King of Tripura, had a first-hand experience of the just Akbar and the wise Birbal.

Story 48

The Scared Harem

The Mughal Emperor went on many hunts. During one hunt, he noticed a pregnant tribal woman in the jungle. Before his very eyes, he saw her enter a bush. Worried about her safety, he stayed nearby.

Some minutes later, he heard a baby cry. Within a minute, the woman came out from the bush with a baby in her arms! Akbar was amazed. In his harem, pregnant women had over a dozen attendants. There were many doctors. Not to mention wet nurses, who fed the child and looked after it. But here, this tribal system was truly amazing.

On returning to the city, Akbar ordered that all women in his harem would deliver naturally. There would be no "artificial" medical attention, henceforth.

On hearing this, all the begums were most worried. Many of them would die while giving birth, they feared.

Naturally, they all approached Birbal. He told them to stop worrying. He would ensure the order was never carried out.

A few weeks after his strange order, Akbar was strolling in the royal gardens. As he looked around, he was shocked. All the rose plants and trees had turned dry and died. He had grown these plants with such tender care. Akbar was sad and very angry as well. He quickly summoned the gardener. Instead of going to the Emperor, the gardener rushed to Birbal.

Both then went to the Emperor. "How did all these plants die?" the Emperor bellowed.

"Sire, we have simply followed your order about stopping all 'artificial' medical and other attention," Birbal replied. "In the forests, no plants or trees are watered or looked after. They still survive, don't they? So why must roses in the royal gardens be pampered?"

The stupidity of his own decision quickly struck Akbar. He immediately cancelled his order that denied medical attention to pregnant women in his harem. Within weeks, the rose plants in the royal garden were blooming once again.

Akbar's Strange Dream

Many times, the Badshah had strange dreams. Akbar once dreamt he had lost all his teeth, except one. The next morning, all the astrologers were summoned to the Court. Akbar asked them to interpret his dream. The man who did so correctly would be rewarded.

All the astrologers had long discussions. They then told Akbar that all his relatives would die before him. Akbar got very upset with this interpretation. He asked all the astrologers to leave the Court empty-handed.

Birbal came to the Court late that day. When he entered, he noticed Akbar's sad expression. "Sire, what's the matter? Why are you so sad?" Birbal inquired.

Akbar told Birbal about his dream. "There's nothing to worry, *Jahanpanah*," Birbal replied. "It only means you will live longer than all your relatives. And achieve the most in life."

114

"Birbal, you never fail to answer me correctly," Akbar congratulated his minister. As promised, Akbar richly rewarded Birbal for an accurate interpretation of his dream.

One God, Different Names

The Emperor was once in a very thoughtful mood. "Is anything the matter, Sire?" Birbal inquired.

"Not at all, Birbal," Akbar replied. "I was just thinking about something. We Muslims worship Allah. Christians believe in Christ. Buddhists have Buddha. Various other religions have a God of their own. But Hindus worship so many gods. Why is this so?"

Birbal replied: "*Jahanpanah*, God is actually one. Even for Hindus. He is simply referred to by different names."

The Emperor shook his head: "How is this possible? How can one God assume different forms and yet be one and the same?"

"Why not, Sire? Let me explain," Birbal responded.

The wise minister summoned a man wearing a turban. Pointing to it, he asked: "What's this?"

"A turban, *huzoor*!" the man replied.

"Fine! Now untie it, roll it and tie it around your waist," Birbal commanded.

The man did as told. "Now what is it?" Birbal asked.

"Why, Sir, now it's a cummerbund!" the man couldn't understand what the wise minister was up to.

"Okay! Untie it and wrap it around your waist. That's fine. Now what's this?" he asked.

"It's a dhoti, Sir," the man replied.

"Great! Next, wrap it loosely around your shoulders. That's right. Now what would you call it?" Birbal continued.

"Why, Sir, this is a shawl," the man wondered when this would end.

"Perfect! Now drape it around your neck..." Birbal said, but was cut short by the Emperor.

"Birbal, I've got your point!" Akbar was truly astonished at the simplicity of Birbal's explanation.

"*Jahanpanah*, the cloth in every instance remained just the same. Yet, it was called by different names. That's simply because the user or the usage changed. This happens with water too. It is water vapour in the sky or clouds. It is rain when it falls to earth. It is a river when it flows. It is ice when it freezes. But the central element is one and the same.

"Likewise, God is one and the same. It is only the worshippers who are different. So each person or religion calls God by different names," Birbal concluded.

For once, the entire Court broke out into genuine applause. Emperor Akbar and every person in the Court clapped in recognition of Birbal's unquestioned wisdom. Birbal was truly the most sparkling of Akbar's *Nav Ratnas* or Nine Jewels.

Selected & Retold by
CLIFFORD SAWHNEY

The Funniest Tales of
Mullah Nasruddin

The wittiest stories of the
world's best-loved jester

The Funniest Tales of
Mullah Nasruddin

—Clifford Sawhney

₹ 72/- • Pages: 14

The wittiest stories of the world's best-loved jester

Mullah Nasruddin is undoubtedly the best-known trickster in human history. In some tales, Mullah is the smart joker taking others for a ride. In other stories, he's the one who becomes a fool. In yet others, the joke swings both ways and one isn't exactly sure who has fooled whom! Many tales are awash with unabashed nonsense and unbridled humour – where Nasruddin plays the wise man, the fool, the victim or the prankster in turns!

For centuries, Nasruddin has been amusing people throughout the world. Indeed, Mullah's popularity was universally acknowledged when UNESCO declared 1996 as Nasruddin Hoja Year. His anecdotes are now being spun in modern avatars, with many tales of Mullah's exploits in America and England. This book deals with his tales of yore. After every tale, the author has added a creative insight. No matter what Mullah Nasruddin is called – a wise fool or a foolish wise man – there's no doubt he is the world's most loved trickster.

UNICORN BOOKS

H.O: F-2/16, Ansari Road, Daryaganj, New Delhi-110002
Branch: 23-25, Zaoba Wadi, Thakurdwar, Mumbai-400002

Website: www.unicornbooks.in • **E-mail:** info@unicornbooks.in